rainbow

ANNUAL 1991

This book belongs to

Laura Jane pollock

KU-165-639

£4.25

Contents

Writer: Michael Butcher
Artwork: RWS Graphics

Copyright © 1990 Thames Television Limited.
All rights reserved. Published in Great Britain by
World International Publishing Limited,
an Egmont Company, Egmont House, PO Box 111,
Great Ducie Street, Manchester M60 3BL.
Printed in Italy.
ISBN 0 7235 6875 8
1st Reprint

Decorating the tree

"There," says Geoffrey. "The Christmas tree is ready to decorate now. I'll go and fetch the fairy lights."

"While I'm looking for them you can make a start on the tree with these," says Geoffrey. He hands out three small boxes.

Bungle opens up his box first. "Ooh, these coloured balls will look good on the tree," he says, hanging them on it.

George pulls a long piece of tinsel out of his box. "What a pretty colour," he smiles. Zippy looks in his box, too.

"Do you want to put your things on the tree next?" George asks Zippy. "It's all right," says Zippy. "You go first, George."

George decorates the tree with lots of pieces of tinsel. "That does look nice," he says. "Come on, Zippy, it's your turn!"

"**CHOMP!** All right George," mumbles Zippy. His box was full of chocolate snowmen, but he's eaten half of them!

"I had to find something to do while I was waiting for you two to finish hanging your things on the tree, didn't I?" laughs Zippy.

Super Bungle flies again

Bungle often dreams about flying through the air as **Super Bungle** — the bravest bear in the world! This is what he thinks it would be like. Can you see something else flying in this picture? Join the dots to find out what it is.

Answer:
There is a **hot-air balloon** in the sky.

Zippy

Going underground

Geoffrey has brought Bungle, George and Zippy on a daytrip to London.

"Look at all the **giant** shops here!" says George. "I've never seen so many in one place before."

"There are lots of big shops in London, George," explains Geoffrey. "I think we could all spend days shopping here, don't you?"

"Oh, no!" groans Zippy. "I thought we came here to see the sights — not to do boring old shopping!"

"Don't worry, Zippy," laughs Geoffrey. "We're not going shopping. We're going to **Buckingham Palace** next. We should be there in time to see the **changing of the guard**. Come on, we have to go this way ..." Geoffrey leads them to a small building up the road.

"Is this Buckingham Palace, Geoffrey?" asks Bungle. "It's not as big as I thought it would be. I thought that the Queen lived here, but there aren't any guards!"

"Silly Bungle-Bonce!" interrupts Zippy. "This **isn't** Buckingham Palace! Look at that sign ... it says **Oxford Circus** on it! Geoffrey has brought us to the circus."

"No I haven't," laughs Geoffrey. "This is an **underground** station. It's just called Oxford Circus because it's on Oxford Street and lots of train lines meet here. We're going to catch an **underground** train from here to where Buckingham Palace is." Geoffrey takes his friends into the station and buys four tickets for the train.

"Where do we have to go now?" Bungle asks Geoffrey. Geoffrey shows him a special map on the wall that has lots of coloured lines on it.

"We have to go along this **blue line** here," says Geoffrey, pointing to a line on the map. "That means we have go that way now, down there! Now be careful on the steps — and stand still on the right hand side!"

"**Huh!** What's the use of just standing still on the steps?" scoffs Zippy. "We'll never get to the bottom . . .

YIKES! They're moving!"

"Ha, ha! I know what this is. It's an **escalator**, isn't it, Geoffrey?" chuckles George.

"That's right, George," says Geoffrey. "Now all of you hold on to the handrail until we get to the bottom." When they get there, Geoffrey leads the way to the platform. It isn't long before a train arrives.

"Hmm," says Bungle, when he sees the train. "You must have brought us to the wrong place, Geoffrey!"

"What do you mean?" Geoffrey asks Bungle.

"Well, you said we were going along a **blue** line," explains Bungle. "This platform isn't blue and the train isn't either. We must have gone wrong somewhere!"

"This line is only blue on the map, Bungle," laughs Geoffrey. "The train isn't actually blue. Now hurry up, everyone! We have to get on the train before it sets off again. They don't stop for long you know!" They all get on board and Zippy spots three empty seats, all together. Bungle, George and Zippy sit down, but there's no seat for Geoffrey!

"Oh, dear!" says George. "There's no room for you on this train, Geoffrey. You'll have to catch the next one. What are we going to do without you? We won't even know which stop to get out at."

"Don't panic, George!" Geoffrey tells him. "I wouldn't dream of leaving any of you on your own in the middle of London. I don't have to sit down to stay on this train. I can stand up and hold on to this rail. Lots of people stand on underground trains!" It's not long before they reach the station where they have to get off the train.

"That sign says the **way out** is this way," says George, leading his friends up the platform, when they have all got off the train. "**Ah-ha!** And over there must be the escalator we have to go up." But when George reaches the escalator he has seen, there are lots of people coming **down** it! "Oh, no!" he gasps. "If we're trying to go up, but the stairs are moving down, it'll take us hours to get to the top! We may never make it.

Then we'll be trapped underground **forever!**"

"It's all right, George," laughs Bungle, pointing to another escalator. "This one's going up. I think this is the one we're meant to use!"

"Thank goodness for that," George sighs with relief, as they head for the top. He is very pleased when they finally come out of the underground station into the fresh air. "Ah, that's better," he says. "It's good fun having a ride on the underground, but I think I like being **overground** much more!"

Bungle's new face

Bungle was trying to draw a picture of himself, but he just couldn't get it right. Then he had an idea — why not trace his own face on to a large piece of paper with a felt tip pen? Of course, he couldn't see what he was doing, so the picture did look very funny!

Would you like to draw a picture of yourself, just like Bungle did? It's easy, just do the same as Bungle, but do be very careful not to get felt tip all over yourself!

George dives in

"Dive, dive, dive!" chuckles George, playing with his toy submarine in the bath. "Up periscope, Captain!"

"I wish I was the captain of a **real** submarine," says George, thinking hard about what it would be like . . .

Captain George inspects the crew of his submarine. "Very good, men," he tells them. "Now get back to work!"

"Hmm," thinks Captain George, looking around his submarine. "These walls really could do with brightening up."

Captain George finds his crew and tells them to start painting the walls. "This bright pink colour will be nice," he says.

"Oh, yes," says Captain George, later on. "That's much better! You've done a good job, Mister Geoffrey. Well done!"

"I know just how to finish it off," says Captain George. "Here, Mister Geoffrey, nail this picture to the wall!"

"I don't think that would be a good idea, Captain," says Mister Geoffrey. "Just do as you are told!" orders Captain George.

So Mister Geoffrey tries to knock a nail into the wall of the submarine. "Oh, no! It's gone right through!" he gasps.

Soon the water comes gushing in through the hole! "**Help! Help!**" cries Captain George. "My submarine is sinking!"

"**Glub!**" says George, as water trickles all over his head, waking him up from his daydream. "Hurry up!" says Bungle.

"It's my turn for a bath," says Bungle. "**Phew!**" sighs George. "My submarine **hasn't** sunk!" Bungle is very puzzled!

Wobbling along

George likes all kinds of underwater animals. He's made up this funny rhyme about a jelly fish. Can you say it with him?

I'd like to be a jellyfish,
And wobble through the sea,
I'd wobble off for miles and miles,
Then wobble home for tea!

Putting you in the picture

You all know what Bungle, George, Zippy and Geoffrey look like, and now they know what quite a few of you look like, too! Here are some of the many Rainbow fans who have sent us their photographs . . .

This is Kimberley Joy Fitchett of Harrow, Middlesex. Her mum ironed her special Rainbow transfer on to a tracksuit for her. Doesn't it look great?

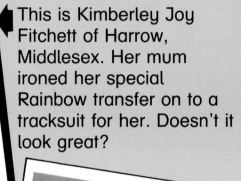

Here's Joel Hartley with two of his very best friends! Joel comes from Southampton in Hampshire.

Christina Shopland of Saughall, Chester is making a wish on her birthday. Her mum and dad made her a smashing Rainbow cake!

Victoria Bowden of Enfield in Middlesex collects everything she can find to do with Rainbow. Here she is with some of her favourite comics, badges and videos!

Rebecca Lee was delighted when her Aunty Sharon made her this super Rainbow jumper. Rebecca lives in Newark in Nottinghamshire.

This is Lee Kelly of Dartford, Kent. He loves to sing along with Rainbow when it is on television and he always enjoys reading the Rainbow Comics and Annuals.

Gus's giant problem

Gus the giant was fed up. Being a giant was just no fun at all! Whenever it rained he always got wet through, because he could never find anything big enough to shelter under.

"I can't even make any friends," he thought, miserably. "Every time I go up to say hello to anyone, they run away. They're all scared of me because I'm a giant." Poor Gus had to make all his own clothes, too. It was the only way he could get them big enough to fit him!

Then, one day, as Gus was walking past a small village, he heard a little girl crying.

"Oh, dear," thought Gus. "She must be crying because she's scared of me. If only I could explain . . ." So Gus went over to the little girl, but she wasn't scared of him at all. In fact, she hardly noticed he was there at first! "What's your name, little girl?" asked Gus. "And why are you crying?"

"H-hello, Mr Giant," sobbed the little girl. "My name's Lesley and my little cat, Skookie, is stuck up that tree. I just don't know what to do!"

"Ho, ho!" laughed Gus. "Is that all?" He walked over to the tree and picked Skookie out of it. "Here you are, Lesley," he smiled. "Your cat . . . safe and sound!"

"Ooh, thank you, Mr Giant," said Lesley.

"Please call me Gus," said Gus. He was happy to have found a friend at last. "You know," he laughed, "sometimes being a giant does have its good points, doesn't it?" Lesley and her pet cat both had to agree!

Stormy weather

This time Gus has been caught in a really bad rainstorm. Luckily he's found an extra-large tree to shelter underneath until the rain stops. Can you spot five differences between these two pictures of him trying to keep dry?

Answers: 1. A branch has disappeared from the tree; 2. A storm cloud has moved; 3. The door of the house has changed colour; 4. Gus's foot has moved; 5. Another bird is sheltering under the tree.

Bungle

Zippy's indoor garden

"Oh, no!" groans George. "Look at all that rain! I wanted to go outside and do some gardening today." "Don't worry," Geoffrey tells him. "We'll do some gardening **indoors!**" "Indoors?" gasps Zippy. "We can't do any gardening indoors, Geoffrey. We'd have to dig the carpet up!" "No, we won't," laughs Geoffrey. "I'll show you what we can do . . ."

Geoffrey fetches the pineapple they are going to have after dinner and cuts about 3cm off the top of it. "We could do just the same with the tops of carrots or turnips," he tells the others. Next he puts the pineapple top in a saucer of water. "Now all we have to do is keep the saucer topped-up with water and wait," says Geoffrey. "In about a week, leaves will sprout out of the top and we'll have our own indoor pineapple plant!"

Then Geoffrey gets an onion and he fills an old jam jar almost up to the top with water. Next he pushes four cocktail sticks into the middle of the onion and puts it on the jam jar. "We can watch how the onion grows," he explains to Zippy and George. "We'll be able to see it sprout at the top and watch its roots growing down into the jar, as long as we keep it full of water." Finally, he puts both the onion and the pineapple on the windowsill.

"I like this indoor garden," Zippy tells Geoffrey. "It's easy to look after." Just then, George notices that the rain has stopped. "Come on," he says. "We can go out now and do some work in the outdoor garden." "It's all right," says Zippy. "I think I'll stay right here and keep an eye on this one!"

Tiddlywinks

"**Hee, hee!** I nearly got it in that time!" laughs George. He is playing **tiddlywinks.** He and his friends take it in turns to try to flick their tiddlywink into a small cup in the middle of the table.

"Right!" says Bungle. "It's my turn now. I'm still a long way from the cup, so I'll try an extra-strong flick . . ." **PING!** Bungle's tiddlywink flies up into the air and right off the table!

"**Ha, ha!** Trust Bungle-Bonce! You missed by a mile!" sniggers Zippy. "You just don't know how to play this game. I'm the best at tiddlywinks in this house!"

"Oh, do be quiet, Zippy!" shouts Bungle. "Come and help me find my tiddlywink on the floor."

"**Ha!**" snorts Zippy. "I don't see why I should help you. After all, I'd never do anything as silly as lose my tiddlywink in the first place!" he says, running off to the kitchen to pour himself a cool drink of lemonade.

"Don't worry," says George. "I'll help you find your tiddlywink." They look all over the room for it, but it's nowhere to be seen.

"**Ah-ha!** I've found it!" says Bungle at last. His tiddlywink had rolled right under Geoffrey's favourite

armchair! "Now we can get back to our game. It's your turn now, George. I'll have to start again." George flicks his tiddlywink very carefully and it jumps into the cup.

"**Hooray!**" he shouts. "I did it! I won!" Just then, Zippy comes back into the room with his lemonade.

"I'll play you now, George," says Zippy, putting his drink down on the table. "I'll go first . . ."

Zippy flicks his tiddlywink, but it doesn't go very near the cup. Next George takes his turn and his lands closer.

"Now then," says Zippy. "I'm sure to get it in this time. My first shot was just a practice shot, you know." He lines up his shot carefully.

"Hmm . . . perhaps a little bit to the left . . ."

"Hurry up!" says Bungle. "I'd like to play another game before bedtime, Zippy!"

"All right, all right," Zippy tells him. "I'm ready now. I just want to make sure I don't miss!" He takes aim and flicks his tiddlywink . . . right into his drink of lemonade!

"**Ha, ha!** What a good shot!" laughs Bungle. "But, Zippy, didn't you know you're supposed to aim at the **cup**, not your **beaker?**"

"**Humph!**" moans Zippy. "You put me off, Bungle!"

"Never mind," chuckles George, picking up Zippy's beaker of lemonade and looking at the tiddlywink inside it. "We can play a new game now . . . tiddly**drinks!**"

Animal question time

This is a game to play at a party or just with some of your friends. First you'll need pictures of animals — perhaps you could cut some out of a magazine, or you could simply draw them yourself. Next, each player must have an animal picture stuck to their back with sticky tape. It may be best if you ask a grown-up to help you with this. You are not allowed to see which animal picture has been stuck to your back! Then you have to guess what kind of animal you are by asking your friends questions about yourself. They can only answer yes or no and you're not allowed to ask things like "am I a lion?" — you have to ask things like "do I have a tail?" or "am I furry?" until you're sure you know. When you do guess, you must pretend to be the animal. If you're right you win the game!

The wash-out

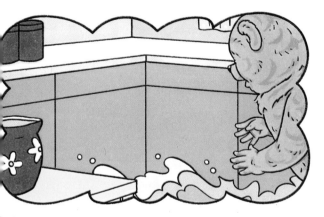

"Geoffrey!" shouts Bungle, one afternoon. "Come quickly! The kitchen's flooded. There's water everywhere! Look!"

"Oh, no!" groans Geoffrey. "Trust Bungle-Bonce to make a mess," laughs Zippy. "It wasn't me!" says Bungle.

"Has it been raining a lot, Geoffrey?" asks George. "No," sighs Geoffrey. "The washing machine has broken down."

Geoffrey mops up the water. "Now we'll have to take our clothes to the **launderette**," he tells his friends.

Bungle, George and Zippy get ready, then Geoffrey takes them and his washing to the launderette in town.

Zippy is the first one into the launderette. "Look at all these televisions!" he says. "I've never seen so many!"

Zippy sits down. "This isn't a very interesting programme, Geoffrey," he says. "Could you switch over for me?"

"Silly Zippy!" says Bungle. "They aren't televisions! They're washing machines, just like ours at home, but bigger!"

"That's right," says Geoffrey, putting washing powder in the machine. "We'll have to use these until ours is mended."

"I'll turn the machine on," says Bungle. He presses a button, but nothing happens! "Oh, no! What's wrong now?" he gasps.

"It's no good, Geoffrey!" groans Bungle. "This washing machine is broken, just like the one at home!" Geoffrey smiles.

"I'm afraid that, unlike our machine at home, we have to put money in this one to make it work," laughs Geoffrey.

The land before time

Have you ever heard of **dinosaurs?** They lived a very long time ago, long before there were any people. Do these three dinosaurs look like anyone you know? Geoffrey is sure that he's seen them somewhere before! There's a **Zippiosaur**, a **Georgadactyl** and a **Stegabungle!** Can you guess which is which?

How many **rocks** can you see in this picture?

6

How many **trees?**

3

How many **clouds?**

4

How many
small dinosaurs?

 3

How many
lakes?

Answers:
There are **6 rocks, 3 trees, 4 clouds, 3 small dinosaurs** and **1 lake** in the picture.

Titch times two

"Hmm . . . just what I'm looking for," said Titch the Mouse, licking his lips. He was in Geoffrey's kitchen and he'd just found a big chunk of cheese!

"This will do for dinner tonight," thought Titch, carrying it back to his mouse-hole. But, just as he was almost home, Titch found that he couldn't move his feet at all!

"Yuk!" groaned Titch, dropping his cheese. "What am I standing in?" He was stuck in some plasticine which Zippy had dropped earlier on! Slowly, Titch pulled his feet free.

"This is funny stuff," said Titch, rolling up the plasticine into a ball. "I think I'll keep it." He picked up his cheese and took that and the plasticine into his hole. Then he had a funny idea. He pushed and pulled the plasticine. Then he prodded it a bit. At last, he had finished. He had made a plasticine model of his piece of cheese!

"It looks almost good enough to eat," laughed Titch. "I won't eat it, though, because I've already got that nice, tasty piece of cheese for dinner. Hee, hee!" Just then, Titch noticed a small piece of paper on his doormat.

"I wonder what that is?" he thought, rushing over to find out. He picked it up and read a message written on it: "Dear Titch . . . see you later for dinner – your friend, Cuffy."

"Oh, no!" groaned Titch. "Cuffy means well, but he never stops talking. Every time he comes round for dinner he nearly talks my ears off! And we don't get around to eating for hours and hours." Titch could already feel his tummy rumbling. "Oh, dear," he thought. "I can't wait all night for my dinner. I'll be starving! There must be something I can do, but what?"

Then Titch realized that there was something he could do. He went over to his plasticine model and rolled it into a ball. Then he pulled it into two round shapes – one big and one small.

"I'll make the head first," he said, looking in the mirror.

He took the small piece of plasticine and shaped a little mousey nose on it, then some big mousey ears! Soon this was finished and he started on the big piece. He pulled hard to make two mousey legs, then he made two mousey arms as well! Finally he put the two pieces together.

"Just one more thing," said Titch, picking up a small piece of plasticine that he had saved. He rolled it into a long sausage shape and put it on his model. "There," he smiled. "Now it has a tail. My model Titch is complete!"

"Hello! Is anyone there?" came a voice from outside.

"Uh-oh!" thought Titch. "Looks like I finished just in time. Cuffy's here!" He put his model in the middle of the room and hid behind the sofa. "Come in, Cuffy!" he called.

"Ah, there you are, Titch," said Cuffy to the model Titch. "I've got so much to tell you . . ."

As Cuffy was chatting away to the model, the real Titch sneaked out of his mouse-hole for some peace and quiet . . . with his chunk of cheese, of course!

"He'll never notice that isn't really me," Titch chuckled. "Once Cuffy starts talking nothing can stop him!"

Rainbow star portrait

Geoffrey

37

Hungry Zippy game

Zippy can be very greedy, but even he wouldn't like to eat ping-pong balls! In the Hungry Zippy game that's just what you have to "feed" him to win!

You will need:
A large cardboard box
Paints, felt pens, or crayons
Round-ended scissors
Ping-pong balls

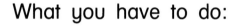

What you have to do:

1. Take the large cardboard box and draw a big Zippy face on it with an extra-large mouth! Don't forget to draw Zippy's zip on the right hand side of his mouth.

2. Ask a grown-up to cut out Zippy's mouth for you.

3. Now colour in the box with your paints, crayons or felt pens. You might make a bit of a mess, so don't forget to put down plenty of old newspaper before you start.

4. Now your Hungry Zippy Game is ready. Stand well back and try to throw ping-pong balls into Zippy's mouth. If you're playing with a friend, the winner is the one who gets the most in. Bungle and George both think it's a great game!

Doctor Zippy

"What's this, Geoffrey?" asks George, looking through some of his old toys. "It's a toy **stethoscope**," says Geoffrey.

"A stethoscope?" says George "Is that something that you liste to music on?" he asks. "Sill Georgy!" says Zippy.

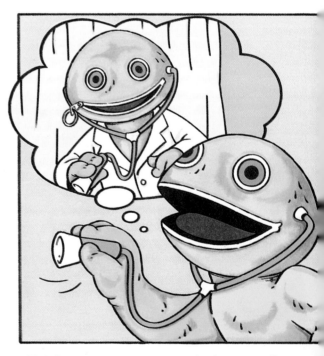

"I know what a stethoscope is," boasts Zippy, taking it from George. "Doctors use them to listen **inside** you with!"

"I'd be a very good doctor," say Zippy. "I could use m stethoscope to find out what wa wrong with people . . ."

"**ZIPPY!**" shouts George down he stethoscope. "Can I have a jo?" "Ouch!" says Zippy. "There's no need to shout!"

"Wait," says Zippy. "I have an idea for a game we can play!" He calls Bungle, then they all rush off upstairs.

They go into the bedroom. "Right, George," says Zippy. "You hide a clock under the bedcovers and 'll try to find it."

"I'll listen for its ticking with the stethoscope!" adds Zippy. "This should be fun," chuckles George.

"**Ah-ha!** I can hear it ticking already!" boasts Zippy. "TICK-TOCK! TICK-TOCK! Am I getting warm yet, George?"

Suddenly, there is a loud noise from under the covers. **RING RING!** "**Oww!**" cries Zippy, jumping with surprise.

"Ow! What a noise!" says Zippy, pulling the clock from under the bed covers. "This is an **alarm** clock," he gasps.

"I'm sorry, Zippy," smiles George. "It was the only clock I could find. I didn't think you'd be so **alarmed** by it!"

What do they need?

All the people on this page need special equipment to do their job. Can you match the people on the left with the things that they need on the right?

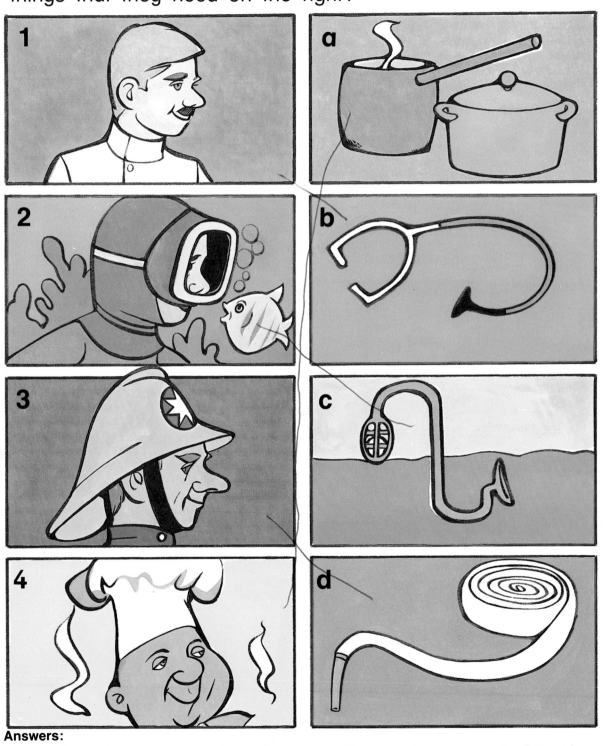

Answers:

1 (a doctor) matches with **b** (a stethoscope), 2 (a diver) matches with **c** (a snorkel), 3 (a firefighter) matches with **d** (a hose), 4 (a chef) matches with **a** (cooking pots).

43

rainbow art gallery

Many of you have sent us your pictures through the Rainbow Comic. Here are some of the very best ones . . .

Caroline Williams of Rottingdean, Brighton, drew this picture of your Rainbow friends. She thinks that Zippy is a big head!

Isn't this a smashing picture of Bungle? It was sent in to us by budding artist Samantha Charvy of Harrow, Middlesex.

Laura Hughes of Wilmslow, Cheshire really loves Rainbow. This is her fantastic picture of Bungle, Zippy and George.

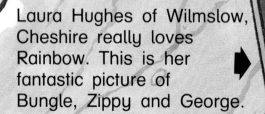

Here's another super picture of the Rainbow gang. Angela Richardson is the artist this time. She comes from Hull in North Humberside.

Zippy must be Darren Thompson's favourite Rainbow character! Darren lives in Bolton Haddington, East Lothian and he's drawn this very colourful picture.

Richard Kennett of Stroud in Gloucester is another brilliant artist. What do you think of his drawing of Bungle, George and Zippy out for a walk in the woods?

Glob, the little green man

Glob was a little green man. He lived on a little green planet far, far away. He even had a little green house in a little green street.

"I wonder why everything around here is the same colour?" he thought one day, as he watered his little green flowers. "I'm sure things would be more interesting if they weren't." So he went out to his little green shed and mixed some paint. But it wasn't **green** paint. . . it was **red!**

"I've been meaning to paint my house for quite a while," he said. "I think I'll paint it red, just for a change!" So he did.

When Glob's friends saw his little red house, they couldn't believe their eyes. "Look at that!" they laughed. "What a funny colour. Silly old Glob! Fancy painting his house red!"

"It-It's not **funny**," said Glob. "It's just **different!** What's wrong with being different?" Glob was proud of his little red house and he didn't care what anyone else thought of it.

It wasn't long before Glob was the talk of the little green town. Everyone wanted to see his house when they heard that he'd painted it red. In fact, it was the most exciting thing that had happened on the little green planet for a long time!

Soon, lots more of the little green people were busy painting their houses new colours. Some of them chose blue, some of them yellow and, in no time at all, there were houses painted in all the colours of the rainbow!

"Ah," thought Glob, looking around the colourful town. "I've really managed to **brighten** up things around here!"

In the box

Hedgehogs for tea!

How would you like to have **hedgehogs** for tea?
Sounds horrible, doesn't it?
Well it isn't when you follow this simple recipe!

You will need:
A tin of pear halves
Flaked almonds
Chocolate chips
Chocolate ice-cream

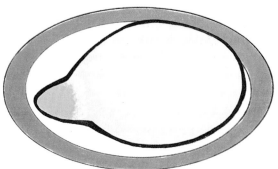

1. Place a pear half on a small plate like this.

2. Stick almond flakes into the pear so that they look like the spines of a hedgehog.

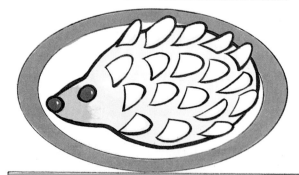

3. Next add small chocolate chips for the hedgehog's nose and eyes.

4. Finally put some chocolate ice-cream in a bowl and then sit your hedgehog on the "ground"!

Your hedgehog is now ready to eat for tea.

On the move

"My friends, Dawn and Andrew, are moving house today," Geoffrey tells Bungle, George and Zippy. "I promised that we'd go round and help them."

"Moving house?" repeats George. "That sounds like very hard work. I don't think I'd be strong enough to pick a house up. How could anyone possibly move one?"

"I didn't mean that my friends wanted to move their house, George," smiles Geoffrey. "They're going to move **out** of their house and **into** a new one!"

"Silly Georgy-Porgy! Fancy thinking you could move a house to somewhere else," laughs Zippy. "That would be impossible!"

"It wouldn't be impossible if Geoffrey's friends lived in a **caravan,** Zippy!" Bungle points out.

"Ah, well, I know that!" says Zippy. "B-but a caravan's not a proper house and, anyway, Dawn and Andrew don't live in a caravan . . . er . . . do they, Geoffrey?"

"Of course not, Zippy," says Geoffrey. "Now, get ready you three. I've just telephoned Dawn to tell her we're on our way." Bungle, George and Zippy put their coats on, then Geoffrey drives them round to Dawn and Andrew's house in his car.

"Look at that **gi-normous** truck!" says Bungle, when they get there.

"That's the **removal van**," explains Geoffrey. "Andrew has hired it for the day to help him take all his furniture and things up to his new house." They get out of the car and Geoffrey knocks on Dawn and Andrew's door.

49

"Good idea," says Geoffrey, going upstairs to help.

"What would you like me to pack away for you, Dawn?" asks Bungle.

"Right," says Dawn. "You and George could start by packing all the books in the living room into a couple of big boxes. Zippy can help me sort out the kitchen."

"I'm very good at packing things, Dawn," boasts Zippy.

"I'm sure you are," smiles Dawn. "You can put all the things on the kitchen table in a box if you like." Zippy packs away the teapot, the kitchen sink drainer and quite a few other things in a box.

"There!" he says. "I'm finished already, Dawn. I bet Bungle and George aren't even half way through filling up their boxes yet!"

"Oh yes we are!" says Bungle, coming into the kitchen with an armful of books. "We've filled up both boxes, but there's no room in them for these . . . **OOPS!**" He trips up on a tea-towel that Zippy has left on the floor and drops the books on the floor.

"Sorry, Dawn!" groans Bungle.

"Ah, come in, Geoffrey," says Dawn. "I'm glad you brought Bungle, George and Zippy with you, too. We need all the help we can get today!"

"Where's Andrew?" asks Geoffrey.

"He's upstairs, getting the wardrobes and the bed ready to bring down and put in the van," Dawn tells him. "Perhaps you could go up and give him a hand, Geoffrey, while I get Bungle, George and Zippy to help me pack up some boxes."

"Never mind," says Dawn. "We'll put these books in Zippy's box. There's still some room in it."

Much later on, after Geoffrey and Andrew have loaded all the furniture in the removal van, Dawn puts the last box in the back.

"I think we're ready to go," says Andrew, climbing into the driving seat. He and Dawn drive up to their new house, while Geoffrey and the others follow in the car. When they get there, they take all the boxes out of the van and put them in the house.

"**Phew!** Before we do anything else, I think we all deserve a nice cup of tea," says Geoffrey. Everyone thinks that is a very good idea, but first of all they have to find the cups.

"Hmm . . ." says Bungle. "I remember packing the cups. I think they're in that big yellow box over there." But when they look through the box they can't find any cups. "Maybe I put them in that little blue box," suggests Bungle. But they're not in the little blue box either!

"Trust Bungle-Bonce to forget where he's put things!" scoffs Zippy. "He'd forget his head if it wasn't stuck on!" After Geoffrey has unpacked **five** boxes, he finds the cups.

"Thank goodness," he says. "Now all we need is the **teapot,** because I've already found the kettle."

"Ah, well, that's all right then," says Dawn. "Zippy packed the teapot, didn't you, Zippy? Where is it?"

"**Ulp!**" says Zippy. "It's in that green box . . . or is it in the orange one? Or maybe . . ."

A puzzling picnic

Geoffrey has brought Bungle, George and Zippy to the country for a picnic. Zippy is already tucking into a sandwich! Can you see Titch the Mouse joining in, too? There are six more very strange things going on in this picture. Can you spot them all?

Answers:

1. There's a cow wearing wellington boots! 2. George has a zip on his mouth, just like Zippy! 3. There's a bottle of lemonade balanced upside-down! 4. A bird is wearing a snorkel and flippers! 5. A tree has feet! 6. Geoffrey is wearing a rubber ring and arm bands!

No escape for Titch

"That's funny," yawned Titch the Mouse, looking at his alarm clock. "It's very dark for this time in the morning." He hopped out of bed and went over to the hole in the skirting board that led to George's bedroom.

"It's blocked!" he gasped. "I can't get out through my front door!" Titch walked around his living room for a while, trying to decide what to do.

"Perhaps I can push my way through," he thought. So he charged at his door and hit it with a big THUD! But it made no difference at all . . . he was still blocked in! Several hours went by and Titch still couldn't think of a way out of his home.

"Oh, dear," he said. "I may be trapped in here forever and I'm already running low on cheese!" Poor Titch just didn't know what to do. Then he heard a faint voice outside his room.

"Come on, George! It's teatime. Don't forget to put your toys away," said the voice. Suddenly, whatever had been blocking Titch's door disappeared and light flooded into his home. He raced over to see what had happened.

"So that's what it was!" said Titch, peering out into George's bedroom. He could see George putting his toybox away.

"Thank goodness," sighed Titch. "Now I can get in and out of my door again. And the first thing I'm going to do is stock up on extra cheese, just in case I ever get blocked in again!"

George

The maze

"I'll soon find my way through here!" boasts Zippy. Geoffrey has brought him and his friends to an outdoor **maze!**

Zippy, Bungle and George g into the maze. They turn lef then right, then left agair "Which way now?" asks Bungle.

"Oh, dear!" worries George. "I don't know. Perhaps there's no way out of the maze! We might be **trapped** here forever!"

"Don't worry, Georgy-Porgy! says Zippy. "I'll find the wa out. You stay here with Bungl I'll come back for you."

A little later, Bungle and George are still waiting. "I wonder where Zippy has got to?" says George.

"Hmm," thinks Zippy. "If I go down here, I'm sure I must be almost out of the maze." He hurries on down the path.

But Zippy hasn't found the way out — he's found his way back to Bungle and George! "Oh, no!" he gasps when he sees them.

"Have you found the way out, Zippy?" asks George. "Er . . . well, not quite, George, but I soon will!" says Zippy.

"Which way should we go then?" asks George. "Er, well, um . . ." stutters Zippy. "That way!" says Bungle, suddenly!

"Come on!" calls Bungle, as he rushes off down the path. "I know the way out of the maze now. Follow me!"

Bungle soon leads them out of the maze. Zippy can't believe it! "How did you know the way, Bungle?" he asks.

"It wasn't easy," grins Bungle, standing on his tiptoes so he can see over the maze wall. "I had to keep on my **toes!**"

Getting out

Bungle, George and Zippy are having another go at finding their way through the maze, but they're lost again. Can you help them find their way to Geoffrey?

How can you keep Bungle, George and Zippy quiet?

...Get them Rainbow Comic every week, of course!

Rainbow Comic

Packed full with stories, puzzles and games featuring all your Rainbow television favourites!

On sale every Thursday

ORDER IT NOW!

Titch the juggler

One day, Titch the Mouse found a piece of old newspaper showing a picture of a juggler at the circus. "That looks fun," thought Titch, so he tried juggling with three pieces of **cheese!** But Titch is not very good at juggling and he soon dropped his cheese – so he decided to eat it instead! Can you put the pictures below into the right order to tell this story?

Answer: The right order is 2,1,4,3.

Silly sounds game

Now you can play the **Silly sounds game!** It's simple, but great fun! All you need are counters, a dice and some friends to play with. Take it in turns to roll the dice, then move the number of spaces that you score. If you land on a yellow square you have to make a silly sound. Try to make it as silly as possible, because if you can make any of your friends laugh then you move on one space. If you can't, then you have to miss a turn! The first one to the finish wins the game. Good luck!

20

22

19

23

18

WOOOOO! like a ghost

17

TICK! like a clock

WHISTLE! like a kettle

15

START

1

2